UNEASY DREAMS

A. R. FISHER

Chapter 1

I had just turned fourteen and my parents were all over me about getting a job. It's like they've been waiting all this time so they can be jerks about a job, besides, what job would hire a fourteen year old anyway.

I got into bed that night looking forward to sleep, but found myself waking up every hour. I couldn't even force myself to sleep after six in the morning. I got up and started the coffee maker.

"Erin, do you know why you need to get a job?"

Here we go again. It's not even light out yet, and she's talking to me again. "Wow mom. You guys yelled at me everyday about getting one. Why don't you just tell me again? Why do I need a job? I'm fourteen, can't drive, not even legal. Would I even be able to get one? Mom, I'm still a kid. I don't want to grow up yet. Not quiet yet. Now I have to get ready for school."

I put my mug filled with coffee on the counter, and went back to my room. I climbed out my window to get to the bus stop.

I was able to take a little nap on the bus, but it wasn't easy.

"Erin, are you okay?"

I looked at Misty. "I had a really bad night."

I turned back to the window. There were thoughts going a hundred miles an hour going through my mind.

⚡ ⚡ ⚡

School wasn't the easiest to get through, but I did it. I took a nap on the way home, but woke with a jump. Misty looked over at me. She smiled slightly out of concern rather than happiness.

When we got to our stop, she helped me off the bus and to my house. "You sure everything is okay?"

That's Misty. Always concerned, always worried, but always knew the truth even if I hadn't told her anything. I lied saying everything was fine and I went inside.

"Thanks," I said closing the door. I looked through the windows curtains and she was still standing there. "I'm sorry."

I went to my room and lay down. My bed felt so comfortable. I closed my eyes and woke refreshed.

I had homework, but didn't want to leave my bed. All I wanted to do was sleep, but couldn't. I grabbed my phone from the front pocket of my backpack and had a message, of course from Misty. She wanted me to call her. I tossed the phone to my bed and went into the living room. My older sister Jaleen was watching her dvr recordings.

"Hey," I said low. "Could I talk to you?"

"Sure." She turned the TV off and faced me.

"Could we talk in your room?"

I sat on her bed. "Were mom and dad like this when you had to get a job?"

"No, and mine wasn't until I was sixteen. They were much more flexible with me."

"Why are they so on me about this? How many places would hire a fourteen year old? The

6

other thing is my sleeping has been way off this week."

"Well you will need a job eventually, but you are right, you are too young for a job. I'll try to talk to them about it, but they aren't to good at listening. Your sleeping sounds like you aren't allowing yourself to relax. Your brain needs a break just as much as your body."

⚡ ⚡ ⚡

I woke from a very familiar dream. I've had this dream before, but never worried about it. The only other time was when gramps passed away and our house was a wreck. Everyone was yelling at each other. Grams moved in with us and every single moment was stressful. My stress has come back because of this job thing. I should just have them kick me out now. I sat up and was still in Jaleen's room. She wasn't in the room. I looked at the clock. It was eight o'clock. I wondered how long I was out for. I opened the door to her room and Jaleen was standing there.

"You're up."

"How long was I out?"

"About three hours."

"I had a dream.

"That's what happens when you allow yourself to relax."

"It's not a good thing," I told her. "I had the same dream when gramps passed away."

"It's nothing Erin."

"It's everything," I said under my breath as she walked away.

Chapter 2

"If I just get a job the stress will subside and the dreams will disappear."

"Erin, who's going to hire you, you're fourteen?" Misty asked.

"I don't know, but my parents are upset because I don't have one?"

"Why?"

"They won't tell me, they just want me to get one."

"Well, what if you get a paper route in the morning."

"I can try."

We talked for a little while longer and said good byes. I hung up and lay down. There was a knock on the door.

"You doing okay?" Jaleen asked.

"Tired, but I'm okay."

"I'll see you tomorrow when I get home? Night."

I got under my covers and felt so warm and comfy.

⚡ ⚡ ⚡

I could hear yelling, but saw nothing but black. I wasn't sure if I was being yelled at. Maybe I am the cause of the yelling, it wouldn't be the first time. Then there was a third voice and the argument became louder.

I woke up screaming at sat up. My door opened and Jaleen flew in. She turned the side lamp on.

"It was only a nightmare." I was catching my breath as I lay back down. She wiped the sweat from my face, and gave me a new shirt.

"It's okay," she said. "I'll stay until you go back to sleep."

I hugged my teddy bear and faced the wall away from Jaleen. She rubbed my back and sang my favorite lullaby.

⚡ ⚡ ⚡

I could hear the lullaby in the darkness. It was very faintly playing in the distance. The lullaby repeated, louder with each playing, and I could hear whispers of arguing. The lullaby grew louder as the arguing got louder. I opened my eyes and looked at my ceiling. I hugged my teddy bear and asked myself what the dreams meant?

After knocking on the door, mom came in and got me up for school. I have a feeling that today was going to be rough.

Chapter 3

Misty sat three seats back and two rows over from me. I could feel Misty keep looking over at me. I looked back to her and saw her start to tear.

"What's wrong?" she asked me in the middle of class.

"Nothing," I said frustrated.

"Nothing," she looked away.

"Would you girls like to take this outside?" the teacher asked.

"No," I said.

Misty left the room with her stuff and quietly closed the door. The teacher looked at me and I looked at the desk. The math problems in my notebook looked like a foreign language.

I sat alone on the bus. I walked alone to my front door. I turned to watch Misty go home.

"I'm sorry," I said.

She stopped walking, and I walked slowly over to her, dropping my backpack on the way over.

"No. I'm sorry. I shouldn't have left the way I did. You're not telling me something?"

"It's this dream."

"What kind of dream?"

"I'm not sure yet, but it's not allowing me to sleep. Well, it does, but I always wake with a jump."

"Someone else I know has the same sleeping pattern. It's been a few months for him though. Has this happened before?"

"Once, and it wasn't this bad."

"Have you ever tried Ouija board?"

"No, I haven't. Why do you ask?"

"Well, that boy, Joey, he has his dreams because of something that is trying to happen. He's fifteen, has a job, and has told me his secret."

"What's his secret?"

"I promised him I wouldn't tell. Come over tonight and well try the Ouija board."

⚡   ⚡   ⚡

I got to her house around seven and we waited until it got dark. She allowed me to nap, which didn't last very long, but it was better than nothing. It was dark when I woke up. The Ouija board was all set up. She had three candles lit by the board and a few others around the room.

"Hey Erin. Are you awake enough to come down? I have to tell you the rules."

"Yeah," I said tiredly and sat up.

"Okay," she said as I moved to the floor.

She explained the rules and we started.

"Can you tell us your name?"

The planchette moved to no.

"Misty, are you moving it?"

"No, I'm not," she said.

"Where are you from?" Misty asked.

The planchette moved to the moon. Then the planchette went to the letters E-R-I-N, and then it moved up to goodbye.

"It spelled my name."

I spent the night with Misty and we slept on the pull out bed from the couch.

⚡ ⚡ ⚡

There was arguing, crying, laughter and fear all rolled into a blackout. I could hear the deep voice laughter. Then I saw the Ouija board float in from out of the darkness, and it spell my name. I saw Misty drift in along with my mom, dad and Jaleen.

My eyes shot open and I sat up. I looked over at Misty and she wasn't there. I was looking into the dark, black room and heard footsteps from the hallway.

"Where did you go?" I asked her.

"To get a washrag."

I lay back down and she sat on the bed next to me.

"What's wrong Misty?"

"Nothing," she said as I saw a tears come to here eyes." Go back to sleep."

"Can't promise I will stay asleep."

Chapter 4

I woke with a jump and it was morning. I stayed awake and went into Misty's room.

"What were you trying to tell me last night?" I was looking at the Ouija board, but nothing happened. "Maybe tonight."

I turned around and felt myself falling.

⚡ ⚡ ⚡

I woke up still in the same spot. I looked to the living room couch and Misty wasn't there. I went around to all the closed doors and I was alone. *Where is everyone?*

I opened the basement door and felt a rush of wind. I opened my eyes and was knocked down by nothing. It hit me again from behind and again from the front.

⚡ ⚡ ⚡

I woke up in Misty's arms still in the hallway. Her mom was there too.

"What happened?"

"You fell?"

"Is that why my head hurts?"

"Yeah," Misty said low.

⚡ ⚡ ⚡

We were sitting in her room, on her bed. I kept looking over at the Ouija board. "What did it mean?"

"What?"

"Last night," I reminded her.

"You do know that the moon spirits are bad."

"I do now. I don't know what to do. I can't sleep anymore. The dreams are getting worse."

"I really think you and Joey should meet," she suggested.

"Is Joey that boy you told me about?"

"Yeah and once I tell him what's going on he might tell you his secret."

⚡ ⚡ ⚡

The arguing is louder than it's ever been and the laughing was trying to overpower everything else. I woke up screaming and a light came on.

"Turn it off," I yelled.

"Hey Erin, Erin. Listen to my voice. Come back. Everyone is here. We are waiting." I could hear her, but I couldn't see her. "Just relax. Everything is okay."

She was looking down at me with a hand on my hand and a hand on my cheek. "There she is."

I felt weight off me as Misty moved off, and onto the bed.

"I'm sorry I woke you up again."

"Hey, we are going to beat this together."

"I can't beat this without Jaleen, but my parents won't understand."

"Maybe you should give them a chance. Maybe they do know what's going on."

"What about us and school?" I asked.

"Luckily we have spring break next week."

"But, what about the rest of this week?"

"We will call in absent. I'm not leaving your side for school, besides it's only two days."

Misty kept me in bed most of the day. Surprisingly, I was able to take a few naps with no nightmares. Her and I went for a walk to the School Park and Jaleen and her friend was there.

"Hey Jaleen," I said while we were walking up the hill.

"How you feeling?" she asked.

"Could be better. Can I talk to you?"

"Sure."

"I have to go anyway," her friend said.

"See you later. What's up," she looked to me.

"The dreams are getting worse," I said. "I can't sleep at night. If I do the nightmare appears. I see a very bad place. It's of our arguments stopping, and being stopped by a very powerful source."

"What kind of source are we talking about?"

Chapter 5

"Mom and dad are hiding something."

"Why would you think that?" Jaleen asked.

"Why else would I be having nightmares like this?"

"Are you going to ask them?"

"Them first, then Joey," I said looking at Misty.

Misty and I sat on the bench with Jaleen. I asked Misty if I could lie on her lap.

I was looking up at the clouds and trees. I felt a refreshing breeze and closed my eyes. I was seeing the clouds within my dream. They were white puffy clouds against a light blue sky. The sky slowly started to spin. It changed its colors from blue and white to red and black. The spinning sped us as if the sky was going down a sink drain. The white eyes came from out of the darkness and so did the creature that the eyes belong to.

I woke up yelling. I heard Jaleen and Misty. "We should go home."

"Fine by me," I said slowly sitting up and catching my breath.

"When are we going to ask them?" Misty asked.

"I'll ask them as soon as I walk through the front door." Jaleen and Misty helped me up and down the hill. From there it was a straight shot to the house. I could feel myself wobbling as I walked. Jaleen kept a hand on my arm. "I'm so tired."

"Once mom and dad know you'll be okay. Just hang in there kid."

"How long do I have to wait after they know?"

Jaleen looked to Misty. "I don't know. Let's just get home."

⚡ ⚡ ⚡

I could see his eyes and his black body coming out of the darkness. He kept coming closer to me. He lifted one arm and slashed openings in my dream.

"No," I yelled as I sat up. My shirt was wet and my breathing was heavy. "I can't, I can't do this anymore."

My door slowly opened and mom and dad came in. "We have something to tell you."

I slowed my breathing and Jaleen and Misty came in and sat on either side of me.

"Erin, the reason we wanted you to get a job was because it would keep your mind busy. Your mind would be less vulnerable."

"Vulnerable to what?"

"Have you ever seen the mark on your back?"

"I always thought it was a birth mark."

"Well, it kind of is, but it's the mark of something else."

"Mom, just tell me what is going on. What is wrong with me?'

"Erin it's my fault. I let it happen."

"Mom. Please just tell me."

She looked down at her hands. "You've been marked by the devil. Through these nightmares he's found a way into your mind."

"Is there a way to get rid of him?"

"I don't know. If only I protected you more."

"When did you know I was marked?"

"The mark itself didn't show up until after your third birthday. Before your third birthday you were a very easy child to deal with. But, there was one night I was giving you a bath and I realized the marking. It looked like a birthmark, so at the time I didn't worry about it. As that year went on your behavior progressively got worse. Your sleep pattern became very weird. I found you walking around the house at night. I found you a few times in the basement asleep on the couch. It was all just very weird. The way we came to the conclusion that it was the devil's mark was of course research. We had a professional come in at night after you had gone to sleep. He didn't even hesitate. He said that it was the devil's mark, showed us a picture, gave us options and apparently we made the wrong choice."

"What choices did he give you? Which one did you chose?" I asked impatiently.

"He gave us the choice of taking it out, or letting it leave on it's own. We made the wrong choice," dad explained.

"So this has been a part of me for eleven years and you choose to tell me now."

"Well, honestly, we forgot about it because after the age of ten you seemed like a normal little girl."

"I'm not normal now. It chooses to take me now."

"It's not going to take you," Jaleen said.

"We have a source," Misty added. "Meet Joey and I promise you won't regret it. This will work."

"When will I meet him?'

"Jeez, we can do it first thing tomorrow."

Mom and dad breathed a sigh of relief and got up. I got their kisses and they left. Jaleen followed them out.

"He's not in school?" I looked to Misty.

"Um, no, I can't tell. He's told me everything, and I promised I wouldn't tell."

"It sounds like he's threatening you."

"No, he's not. I'm not one to break promises. I don't break secrets. Don't you know that by now," she smiled. "Try to go back to sleep. I'll be here if you wake up."

Chapter 6

Misty was by my side, just like she said, but it looked as if she hadn't slept all night. "Did you sleep?"

"No," she said. "I wanted to make sure you didn't have anymore nightmares."

"Can you sleep for me now?"

"If you want me to."

She lay down when I got up. I closed the door behind me when I left. Mom and dad were at the table. They avoided looking at me. I went out back and sat on the porch steps. I was looking out into the green, hilly field behind our house. The trees and woods were a ways back following the horizon line, with dips and hills. The trees and woods were a ways back, but it looked as if a tree was walking forwards.

As it got closer I could see the demon. The demon from my dreams. *Am I dreaming? I don't remember going to sleep.* I waved my hand between my face and this image. He disappeared. I could feel myself breathing again. Short breaths, but it was better than no breaths at all. I felt footsteps on the porch.

"Hun, Erin."

I turned around. "What?"

"Why you breathing so shallow?"

"Bad dream?"

"You slept out here?"

"I just saw him. He was in the field."

"Who darling?"

"Mom, the demon."

"Was it a dream?"

"No, it felt like reality. I don't remember going to sleep."

She got me back to my room and I lay next to Misty, not wanting to wake her. I can't get his face out of my head. I see him ever time I close my eyes. I wanted to sleep so badly, but what's the point if all I see is him. Not again, please, not again.

"Erin," I heard faintly. "Erin, wake up."

"What," I said tired.

"I had to get you out of it. It was another nightmare," Misty said.

"If they would have told me sooner this wouldn't be happening."

"You can't blame them. They were hiding it to protect you."

"You are defending them?"

"Well, yeah."

I was too tired to argue. I sat up. "Where is that Joey kid?"

"He is an absolute last resort."

Why?"

"It's because of the promise. He doesn't want the world to know of his condition."

"So, you're calling this a condition now?"

"Well, that wasn't the right word."

"No, it wasn't."

"Can you please try for sleep," she begged.

"I would love to, but he won't let me."

"Fight him off please."

"I'm trying," I pleaded as I drifted off to sleep somehow.

I opened my eyes and looked around my dark room. I couldn't feel Misty's body next to mine. *Did she leave? Am I scaring her with my nightmares?* I put my feet on the floor and looked out my window. The full moon was giving off a very bright glow through the wispy clouds, and was making three-dimensional shadows on my two dimensional walls. I was looking throughout my room and could have sworn I saw something move in the corner. I looked closer and the white eyes appeared. He came closer and cornered me on the bed, and for the first time he took hold of my arm and tried to pull me off the bed. He had raised his other arm and I could hear myself screaming.

"Erin, Erin," I heard someone yelling. "It's Misty. Wake up."

"I can't," I said but was still in the dream.

"Can't what Erin?"

"Can't come back. He's got me."

"Erin everything is fine. It's okay."

"Misty," I opened my eyes.

"I'm right here."

"You left me?"

"No, I didn't. I was here the whole time.

"It was a dream? I didn't go to sleep?"

"I guess you did."

"He touched me," I said.

"Who?"

"The demon, he touched my arm."

"He has a hold on you now. Yes Erin."

"What does that mean?"

"You seriously need to start fighting back."

"How do I do that?"

"Joey."

Chapter 7

"Go back to sleep," she said,

"Can't, not after that dream."

"Then, I'm staying up with you."

"No, you have a choice. I don't please, you go back to sleep."

"I'm not going to sleep while you suffer."

⚡ ⚡ ⚡

"You need to fight back Erin."

"I can't."

The demon grabbed my arm and lifts his other arm to the ceiling. When his arm tries to hit me, I duck and then jump out my window. I run down the road at the entrance of the cul-de-sac. He never showed back up. I stood in the road, just waiting.

I slowly opened my eyes. "I fought back." I slowly sat up and my room was full of the sun's rays. I though morning would never come. "I fought back."

"Did you?" Misty said.

"I didn't let him do what he wanted to do."

"I guess that's a start," she said. She sat up and looked at me. I'm sure my eyes are unrecognizable. I feel them wanting to close, but my brain is to scared to let sleep happen. I felt her hand on my back. I was able to give her a little smile. "Let's go sit with the family."

"Can I lay on your leg?" I asked.

"Of course you can." She helped me up.

"So, who's this Joey kid?" Jaleen asked.

"He's going to try to help me, but hopefully it will help him too."

"Erin," she said low.

'What? Not even my own flesh and blood?"

"I guess it's okay," she said.

"Joey has been touched by the devil," I say.

"Our goal is to somehow connect her demon and his. Somehow the demons will destroy each other," Misty explains.

"Oh, is that what is going to happen."

"We are going to try."

Chapter 8

I woke up to footsteps on the floor right outside my room. I lay back down and tried to ignore the fact that I was being watched. An open door breaks the darkness and his black figure stands in the doorway.

"Don't let him in," Misty says. "Fight back."

I run towards him, but he shuts the door behind him. I woke up to the slamming door. I look to my door. It was still closed. Misty is asleep next to me.

"Just a dream," I said calming myself down.

"Erin," Misty said tired. "You are awake again."

"Yeah, what difference does it make? I didn't fight hard enough."

"What do you mean?"

"He came in last night. It was through a door I forgot to lock."

"So he is part of you right now?"

"Yeah."

"I'm calling Joey." She got up and dialed his number.

"Why bother? It's the middle of the night."

I lay back down next to Misty, and she sat up. "Joey?"

"Yeah, is this Misty?" She had put the phone on speaker.

"Yup, listen, I need your help with something?"

"Okay?"

"I need you to fight a demon inside of someone I now?"

"You told someone," he said sternly.

"I had to. She had the right to know that she is not alone."

"Want me over now?" he said submissively.

"Could you?"

"Coming," he said then hung up.

Misty looked back at me after hanging up the call. "Go to sleep. Joey will wake you when he gets here."

I wasn't going to argue with her. I could see Misty, Jaleen, mom and dad drifting into the black background. I was trying to hold onto them, but the tighter my grip the harder they were pulled from me. He was getting stronger, as I was getting weaker.

"Don't take them," I begged. I woke up to Misty's scream, and found myself sitting up on bed. "No Joey yet?"

"You were only asleep for a few minutes."

"I'm not going back to sleep. I don't want to lose you or Jaleen," I said.

"You're not going to. Joey will help you."

"So, is this like a special gift he has?"

"Yeah, he calls it a dream bond."

I jumped to the tap on the window. Misty opened it and Joey climbed in. I lay back down and faced the wall.

"How bad?" he asked.

"I can see my family and Misty being taken from me," I said still facing the wall.

"How bad are the dreams?" he asked again.

47

"Well, it started off slow, and is now at the point where the demon is talking through her."

"He has never talked through me," I said turning to look at him.

"It's something we can't feel, but others can see it happen," Joey explained. "What I want to do right now is to trigger the demon. I can't do anything until I know for sure it's a demon."

He pulled me to my back and sat on me. He took the pillow from under my head, and told me to have my arms out to my sides. He then got off me and sat at my head. He then kissed my forehead, then put his thumb where his lips were. His other hand went under my chin. He slightly tipped my head back and he starred into my eyes. I fell into my nightmare and the knob on the door was slowly turning to open. I can't let him in.

"Erin, this is Joey. You have to let everything happen. Don't fight any of it."

"It hurts when I let him in."

"Don't fight it," he repeated with a soft, understanding voice.

The knob was turned and the door opened. Light poured in revealing the demon's black silhouette. I can start to see that everything I loved was being sucked towards the open door. I heard a deep, low, groggy voice. "I will take everything you have. You will have nothing to love, nothing to live for. I will consume you."

I felt a strange energy break free as I came out of sleep. I opened my eyes. Joey was still looking at me, and Misty was still in the room.

I have an idea," Joey said, "but I've never tried it."

"What is it?" Misty asked.

"I can't force him out because he will bring the memories out with him. The only way is to form a dream bond between us and destroy both mine and her demon."

"You've never done it before? How will you know it will work?" Misty asked.

"I've done my research," he says. "But you can't fight it," he said looking at me."

"I will try."

Chapter 9

He laid me on my side, my head on the pillow. "Okay, here is how it's going to happen. The first step is you have to go to sleep. Once you're asleep I will lay next to you. I have to place my hand on your waist. Our foreheads will be touching. Now to make the bond, I have to ask your permission for something."

"Ask away," I said.

"A kiss will allow me to enter and exit your dreams at will, as long as we are touching like this."

"Will this bond remove the demon?"

"Well, my idea was to have our demons meet up and they will destroy each other. It's much easier said than done. Oh, and I'll have to be asleep as well, but I'll still be awake enough to be able to control the dream."

"You sound like a professional." I smiled.

"Let's get you to sleep," he said.

I was lying on the bed. Misty was on the floor and Joey was sitting and swirling on my desk chair. We were having random conversations about everything. Before I knew it sleep had nearly taken over. I was trying to fight it, but then I heard Misty say to let it go. The nightmare didn't start right away, like it usually did. The only thing I could see was black. There was no dream, no nightmare, and no demon.

"Joey," I said awake but my eyes still closed.

"I couldn't find it."

"What do you mean?"

"You weren't dreaming. You were defiantly asleep but I couldn't find the nightmare."

"How do you know that?"

"Because when I went to sleep, there was nothing. It was just black."

"What does that mean?" Misty asked.

"Nothing," Joey said. "We try again tomorrow."

⚡ ⚡ ⚡

It was a beautiful morning, so the three of us sat outside on the swinging seat. Joey and Misty started talking and I had laid my head on his shoulder. He picked his arm up and put it around me. I put my head back on his shoulder and let sleep take me.

"Come on. Where are you?" I yelled.

"You'd think I would go somewhere," he said.

"There you are." Joey would know if I was dreaming or not. "Joey."

"Erin," I heard. "Erin I'm right here."

"Joey."

"Erin, Erin, wake up."

I woke with a jump on Joey's lap. "We should keep you awake until tonight. We can't risk the demon not showing up again.

Chapter 10

We repeated the same set up as last night. He kissed my forehead, then my lips and let me go to sleep.

The demon had grabbed Misty and was dragging her over to the door. The dream zoomed in and I saw the doorframe was a one way ticket to, I don't know where."

"Joey, help her." He didn't show up. Misty was fighting her hardest against the demon's grip. The dream started to blink out, and then it turned into a fuzzy television channel. Another demon blinked into my dream. "Help her."

The demon looked to where I was pointing. He nodded his head and walked over to Misty. "She's mine."

"That's not what I meant," I said. I started to walk over to Misty but hit an invisible wall. "Joey. Uhhh, where is he?"

I could feel that he was with me, but I couldn't find him. Misty had turned her head to look at me. I made eye contact with her and she gave me a vision of what was going on in the real world. I was looking down at my room as if I was on the ceiling. Misty was in the corner trying to cover herself from getting wet. A really bad thunderstorm, with bright lightning, and no thunder, had made its way to our town. The wind had blown open the window and rain was coming in. There I lay motionless and still, with Joey next to me.

I blinked and was back in my own dream watching the two demons dragging Misty over to the door. "Joey, do something."

The demons stopped and looked at each other. "I think I will take her back with me. She will make a wonderful addition to my collection."

"She was mine first."

They both dropped her wrists and the door closed. It looked as if the demons were about to fight. That would defiantly destroy them.

"Don't fight it," Joey said. "Just let everything happen."

The demons had these very strange powers. As they fought each other, I realized they were fighting Joey and me as well. When I saw my demon get hit I could feel more, and more freedom coming back to me, but, my demon wasn't fighting back. Then I remembered Joey saying not to fight it. I wasn't trying to fight it. I wanted to change the dream.

"No," Joey said. "You can't change what goes on in my head. This is all me."

"My demon isn't fighting yours."

"This sacrifice was always meant to be," he said.

I looked to Misty and her eyes were the gateway to the real world. The rain was heavy and the wind was stronger. With every twitch of my body, there was a lightning strike. Joey's body was still while mine looked as if I was in the fight. Misty got up and stood at the side of the bed. She was soaked from hair to shoe. Then, everything became dark, cold and quiet.

Chapter 11

I opened my eyes to see Joey's eyes still closed. I moved my hand to his cheek. "Joey."

"Erin." I looked to Misty. She was still in her wet clothes. Her hair was dripping and her eyes looked heavy. I looked back to Joey.

"Joey, you okay?"

He moved his hand on top of mine. "I'm okay."

"Is your demon gone too?" I asked.

"Erin, my demon is permanent."

"So wait, I don't understand."

"You never will," he said.

"You will never be rid of him?"

"No, Erin."

"Why did you help me then?"

"I believe that no one should suffer the way I am."

"Let someone help you then."

"I can't be helped. It's in my DNA. It runs in my family. He is part of me, not by choice."

"So you are marked, but not like dangerous."

"Do I look dangerous?" he smiled.

"Thank you," I said lightly hugging him.

He smiled and tapped the bed next to him. "Lay back down. You can now sleep without any interruptions."

I looked at Misty. "I'll be back in a minute. I have to get Misty out of her cold clothes." I led her out of my room to Jaleen's room.

As I was leading her to Jaleen's room I realized that the bed wasn't wet but everything else in my room was. Joey and I were dry, but Misty was wet. I guess I won't understand that either.

Jaleen had offered Misty to stay in her room. I was fine with that. I went back to my weirdly dry bed, and lay next to Joey. He was asleep with his demon. I was now worried about him, because I now know his truth. I know why he doesn't tell anyone. He doesn't want people to judge him, or be scared of him. If anyone asks me I find him to be my hero, I just wish I could have done more to help him in return.